Written by Emily Gale

Illustrated by Mike Byrne

First published by Parragon in 2010

Parragon
Queen Street House
4 Queen Street
Bath BA1 1HE, UK

ISBN 978-1-4075-9508-5

Printed in China

JUST JOSIE and the perfect day!

PaRragon

Bath · New York · Singapore · Hong Kong · Cologne · Delhi · Melbourne

This is **JOSIE.**

Her full name is
JOSEPHINE EMILY,
but everyone
just calls her Josie.

She loves rainbows.
clip-clop shoes.
and her little sister Lily

(when Lily's being good).

Lily

Josie

Josie wears a different color every day.
but on special days she dresses like a rainbow.
Josie has drawn a picture of tomorrow.
It's going to be the bestest. most

perfect day ever!

ONE YEAR OLDER!

This is the biggest I've ever been. Now I can do grown-up things like:

CLIMB MOUNTAINS

WEAR CLIP-CLOP SHOES

AND GO TO BED LATE!

Now all Josie needs is **perfect** weather. . . .

But then it all goes WRONG!

It's not fair!

"I promised my friends the most superlicious garden party.

Rain is NOT part of my BIG Idea.

Rain is the WORST thing EVER!"

DEEP BREATH,
COUNT TO TEN.
JOSIE'S GOT A
BIG IDEA AGAIN.

"I'm not letting nasty rain spoil my perfect day."

Josie remembers where rain comes from. Clouds. "I'll just move them!"

But even with ALL of her family blowing really hard from the very top of the house, they can't make them budge.

the rain keeps falling.

Then Josie remembers her manners.
"I know what will work."
says Josie. "I'm going to my
quiet place to speak to the
rain all by myself."

Hello rain.
It's me. Josie.
Can you
please go
away.

Nothing happens, except the rain, which keeps on happening.

DEEP BREATH, COUNT TO TEN. JOSIE'S GOT A BIG IDEA AGAIN.

"If everything else is perfect, this can still be a perfect day."

NUMBER ONE JOB: my hair.

It takes a long time, but finally Josie's hair is

perfect.

NUMBER TWO:
my party clothes.

Because Josie is in such a hurry it takes three tries to get her Mom's clip-clop shoes on the right feet.

clip
clop

clip
clop

ragh!

ragh!

Then she has a big job telling Lily she can't come to her party as a dinosaur.

At last Josie looks **perfect**,
just like a rainbow.

"Red and yellow and pink
and green, purple
and orange
and blue.
I can sing
a rainbow too!"

Josie's new Big Idea
is going well.

UNTIL . . .

BANG! **BANG!** **BANG!**

The beautiful balloons start
popping.
Grandma drops the jello
on the floor.

splat!

Splat!

splat!

Lily starts crying because she hates **LOUD** noises.

Waah!
Waah!
Waah!

And then the telephone rings. . . again. **and again.** **and again.** Mom has some bad news.

ALL of Josie's friends have chicken pox!

Finally the doorbell rings. and Josie's happy that at least one of her friends has managed not to get sick.

IT'S ZAC from next door.

Just when Josie thought that all the WORST things had already happened.

"Why couldn't you get chicken pox?"
Josie asks him.

And Mom yells at Josie. She yells at her on her special day and she has to apologize to Zac.

"It's not fair!"
shouts Josie.

That's it. Josie's
OLD BIG IDEA
and her
NEW BIG IDEA
are completely
RUINED.

She gets Duck
and sits in
the corner.

She DOESN'T WANT any presents.

(Not even that
great big one
over there.)

She DOESN'T WANT to play any games.

(Not even pin the clip-clop shoes on the princess.)

And she DOESN'T WANT any cake.

(Not even if it's made of chocolate.)

"This is the WORST day ever!" Josie says.

The balloons all popped. The jello went **Splat!**

Lily cried—a lot. The only person

who came to my party just

wiped a booger on the cat. And as if

that wasn't bad enough...

IT'S RAINING!

She thinks she's in trouble, but
then Mom smiles and tells her
to look out the window.

Josie can't believe her eyes.

The yellowiest sunshine. . .

the bluest sky. . .

and the most

beautiful

rainbow anyone's

ever seen.

She grabs Lily's hand
and runs outside.

"Here I am on this **perfect** day.

with my very own rainbow...

my best and favorite party clothes...

Mom's clip-clop shoes...

a very chocolatey cake...

and it's even nice to
have Zac here, too.